For lost toys everywhere—
may you be safe and found

First published in the United States of America in April 2014
by Walker Books for Young Readers, an imprint of Bloomsbury Publishing, Inc.
www.bloomsbury.com

Bloomsbury is a registered trademark of Bloomsbury Publishing Plc

For information about permission to reproduce selections from this book, write to
Permissions, Bloomsbury Children's Books, 1385 Broadway, New York, New York 10018
Bloomsbury books may be purchased for business or promotional use. For information on bulk purchases
please contact Macmillan Corporate and Premium Sales Department at specialmarkets@macmillan.com

Library of Congress Cataloging-in-Publication Data
available upon request
ISBN 978-0-8027-3559-1 (hardcover) • ISBN 978-0-8027-3560-7 (reinforced) • ISBN 978-1-61963-896-9 (PJ Library)
092033.4K2/B0702/A3

Art created digitally using Adobe Photoshop
Typeset in Triplex Sans
Book design by Nicole Gastonguay

Printed in China by C&C Offset Printing Co., Ltd., Shenzhen, Guangdong
3 5 7 9 10 8 6 4 2 (PJ Library)

All papers used by Bloomsbury Publishing, Inc., are natural, recyclable products
made from wood grown in well-managed forests. The manufacturing processes
conform to the environmental regulations of the country of origin.

FOUND

Salina Yoon

BLOOMSBURY

NEW YORK   LONDON   NEW DELHI   SYDNEY

One day, Bear found
something in the forest.

Bear thought it was the most
special thing he had ever seen.

He gently carried the toy bunny home.

"This lost Bunny seems sad," thought Bear.
He wanted to help find its home.

With flyers stacked high, Bear set off.

Bear posted flyers on every tree.

were lost, but not a toy bunny.

He searched high . . .

. . . and low for its owner.

But no one came
for the bunny.

Bear wished the bunny was his to keep.

"But the bunny's family must be so worried," thought Bear.

"Poor lost bunny!"

The next day, Bear and the bunny . . .

swung on a tire,

played hide-and-seek,

picked juicy blackberries,

and had a picnic.

It was a perfect day,

until . . .

Bear screeched to a stop.

Bear handed the bunny to Moose.

The bunny was finally going home.

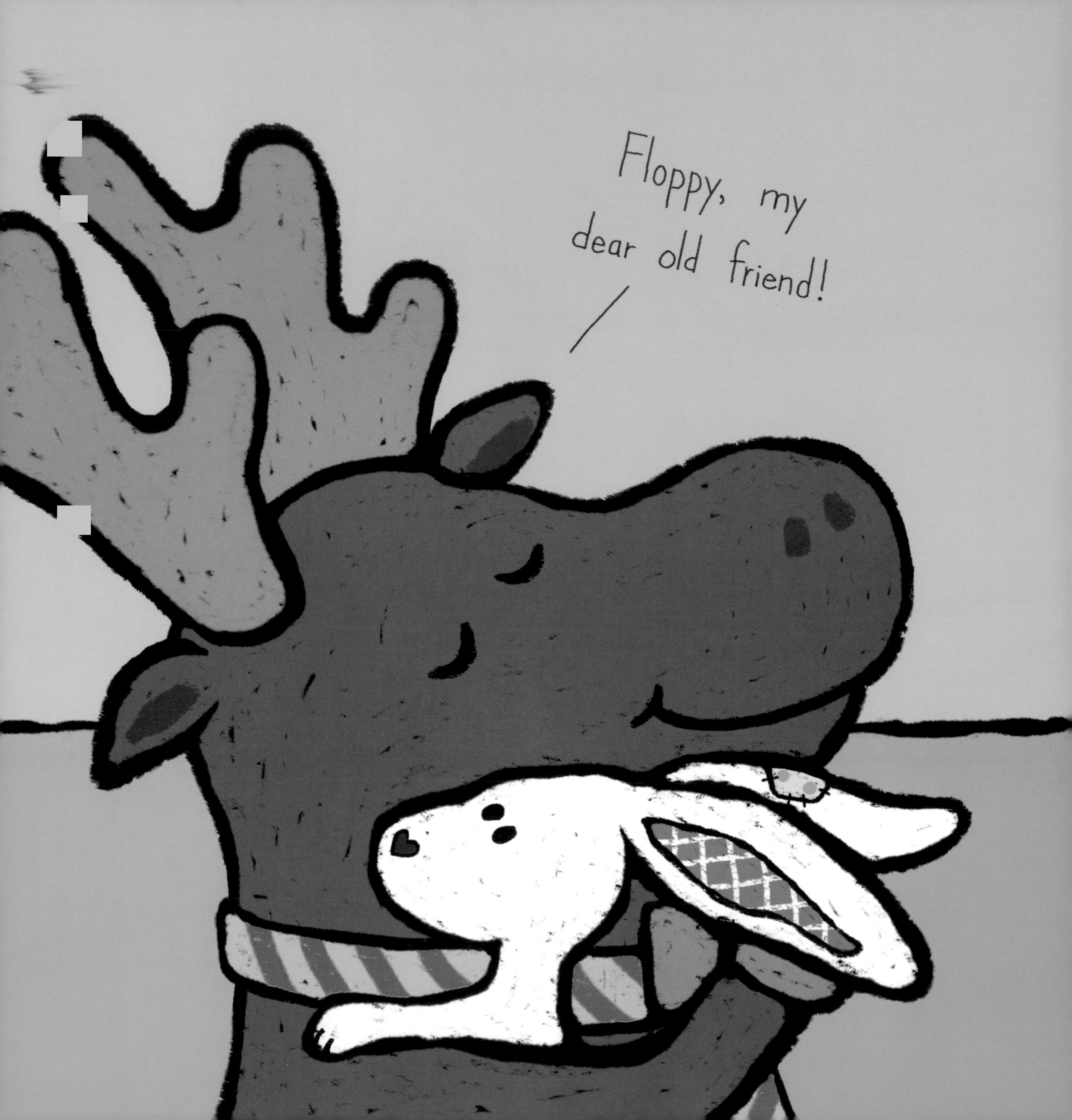
Floppy, my dear old friend!

As a young calf, Moose had
loved Floppy very much.

Good-bye, Floppy.

Moose was glad to see Floppy, but special toys are meant to be passed on to someone special.

"Will you take good care of Floppy for me?" asked Moose.

The bunny wasn't lost anymore.

Floppy was home,
safe and
FOUND!

SALINA YOON has written and
illustrated more than 150 books for
children. She lives in California.
www.salinayoon.com